START YO...

MOTOCROSS CYCLES

By Emma Huddleston

Kaleidoscope
Minneapolis, MN

BIGFOOT BOOKS

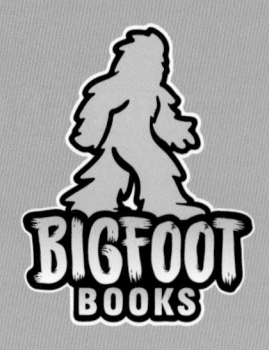

The Quest for Discovery Never Ends

This edition first published in 2020 by Kaleidoscope Publishing, Inc.

No part of this publication may be reproduced in whole or in part without written permission of the publisher.

For information regarding permission, write to
Kaleidoscope Publishing, Inc.
6012 Blue Circle Drive
Minnetonka, MN 55343

Library of Congress Control Number
2019940182

ISBN
978-1-64519-060-8 (library bound)
978-1-64494-218-5 (paperback)
978-1-64519-161-2 (ebook)

Text copyright © 2020 by Kaleidoscope Publishing, Inc. All-Star Sports, Bigfoot Books, and associated logos are trademarks and/or registered trademarks of Kaleidoscope Publishing, Inc.

Printed in the United States of America.

FIND ME IF YOU CAN!

Bigfoot lurks within one of the images in this book. It's up to you to find him!

TABLE OF
CONTENTS

Chapter 1: Racing Hard **4**

Chapter 2: History of Motocross **10**

Chapter 3: Messy Jumps **16**

Chapter 4: Tough Competition **22**

Beyond the Book 28
Research Ninja 29
Further Resources 30
Glossary 31
Index 32
Photo Credits 32
About the Author 32

CHAPTER 1

Racing Hard

Tim brings his **motocross** cycle to the starting line. Its wheels are open. A blue fender sticks out over the front wheel. He climbs onto the blue-and-black seat. He puts his foot on the kickstarter. It's a small metal lever near his right calf. He pushes down hard. At the same time, he gives the **throttle** a quick twist. His bike rumbles to life.

Motocross races start at a gate that drops to let riders through.

FUN FACT
At competitions, racers are sorted into classes based on their age and their bikes' engine size.

He waits for the race to start. His bike rests against a metal gate in front of him. It is the final race of the competition. Tim is at the **Amateur** National Championship. One day, he hopes to be a pro racer.

5

A motocross racer gets the holeshot by reaching the first corner before the other riders.

Tim looks ahead. The gate drops. Vrrrroom! He flies out of the gate. He gets the holeshot! That means he reaches the first corner before the other racers. He turns hard. His wheels push through the ruts in the track.

Mud splatters Tim's goggles. He can barely see. But he doesn't stop. His bike is light and strong. It is built to drive over rough **terrain**. He flies over jumps. He makes the last turn. He crosses the finish line in third place. Tim may not have won. But he's proud of his race.

Tim thinks of Ryan Dungey. He is a former pro racer. Even Dungey didn't always come in first. His amateur career was ordinary. But he took the world by storm in 2010. He won two national titles. If Dungey could do it, so can Tim. Tim keeps working hard. He knows he'll be a motocross star.

Supercross star Ryan Dungey had an ordinary amateur career before his extraordinary pro career.

ZOOM IN ON A
MOTOCROSS CYCLE

Throttle

Front fender

Fork

Engine

Lightweight chassis

Knobby tires

Spokes

CHAPTER 2

History of Motocross

Joe zipped around the track. Dirt flew up around him. It dusted his goggles. It was his first race on his new bike. His old motorcycle didn't do well off-road. It was heavy. It had a rigid frame.

During World War II, many motorcycle models got improvements for easier off-road riding.

This new bike was different. It had been used in World War II (1939–1945). Motorcycles improved during the war. Soldiers needed to get around quickly. And they couldn't always use paved roads.

HOW BIG IS A MOTOCROSS CYCLE?

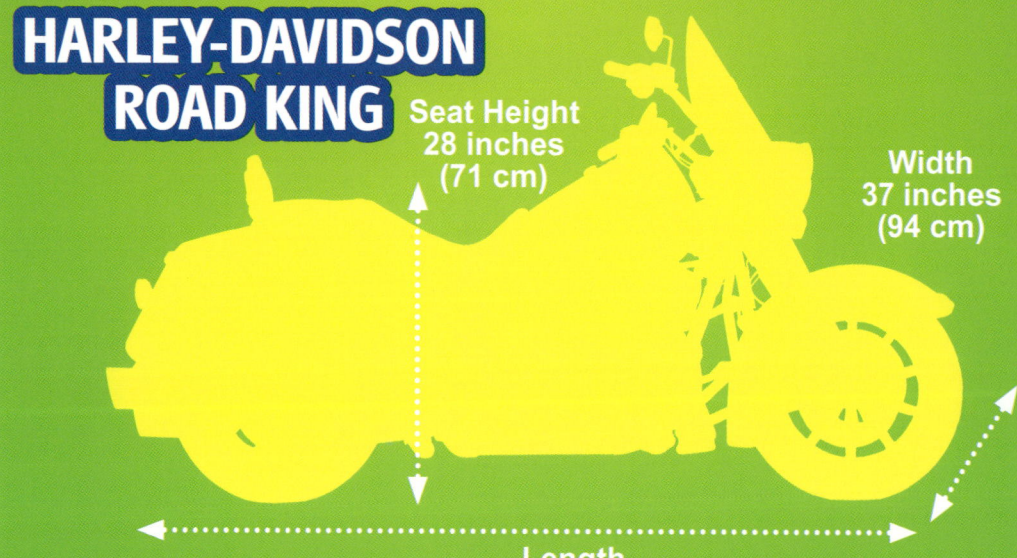

HONDA CRF450R

Seat Height
38 inches
(97 cm)

Width
33 inches
(84 cm)

Length
86 inches (218 cm)

HARLEY-DAVIDSON ROAD KING

Seat Height
28 inches
(71 cm)

Width
37 inches
(94 cm)

Length
96 inches (244 cm)

Motocross racing saw a surge of popularity in Europe after World War II.

Joe's new bike was much better for off-road use. It had a great rear **suspension** system. He rode over a rut in the track. The bike absorbed the shock. Joe saw the finish line ahead of him. He focused and sped past another racer. Joe was first across the finish line!

In the 1960s, Edison Dye went to Europe. Dye saw motocross races. People in the United States raced motorcycles. They even had off-road races. But Dye saw that Europeans did motocross differently.

European motocross was exciting. The athletes were skilled. Their bikes were different from American bikes. They were light but powerful. They were built to go fast over rough dirt courses. Dye brought these dirt bikes back to the United States. He also brought European stars. He organized big races. The stars drew huge crowds. Americans loved the competitions. They wanted to race, too. Dye sold them dirt bikes.

Over time, dirt bikes improved. They went faster. They could handle tougher obstacles. Racers took on harder courses. Updates to motocross cycles are important. They keep the sport exciting.

FUN FACT

The word "motocross" comes from the French word for motorcycle, motocyclette, and the word cross-country.

Thanks in part to Edison Dye, motocross in the United States became the exciting competition we know today.

CHAPTER 3

Messy Jumps

Ricky Carmichael races across the screen. Ava watches his muddy dirt bike flash by. Carmichael is one of the greatest motocross racers of all time. He had two perfect seasons in 2002 and 2004. Ava is inspired. She wants to race motocross, too.

Ava has a dirt bike. Her dad taught her how to ride. She's driven it on trails. Now, she wants to use it for racing. Trail bikes and motocross cycles are similar. They're both meant to ride off-road. But there are some big differences. Ava and her dad get to work.

Trail bikes are similar to motocross cycles, but there are important differences between them.

MOTOCROSS CYCLE STATS:
YAMAHA YZ125

ENGINE SIZE	WEIGHT
125cc	207 pounds (94 kg)
TRANSMISSION	**BASE PRICE**
6-speed	$6,499
TOP SPEED	**SPECIAL FEATURES**
70 miles per hour (112 km/h)	Ultralight aluminum chassis, fast-action clutch, advanced rear suspension for shock absorption and **traction**

17

Ava unscrews the headlight and kickstand. She removes the handguards. These pieces weigh down her bike. She won't need them in a race. Her dad grabs his toolbox. He tightens the suspension. Her bike will absorb impact better. There are lots of jumps and obstacles on the track.

Next, they change the tires. The new ones have big knobs. They'll grip the muddy ground. The bike will get traction through deep dirt. Ava checks the spokes and tire pressure. The tires need to have the right amount of air. Then the tires will have more contact with the ground. This helps the bike go faster.

Ava hopes to get a motocross cycle one day. Her trail bike will work well with some changes. But motocross cycles are designed for racing. They have lighter chassis. And they have more powerful engines. They're built for speed.

FUN FACT
Spokes that are too loose or tight can bend or snap. They can damage wheels.

Small modifications to a trail bike can help prepare it for motocross, but motocross cycles are specially designed for racing.

19

FUN FACT
Motocross bikes only hold about 2 gallons (7.5 L) of fuel.

Succeeding at motocross takes practice, training, and a great cycle.

Ava's bike is ready. Her parents load it into the car. They drive to a track in a nearby town. Ava fills the bike with fuel.

Ava drives through the mud. She leans as she goes around a corner. The tires and suspension keep her steady. She approaches the whoops. Whoops are classic obstacles. They're a series of small hills in a row. The rolling jumps take lots of practice. Carmichael was known for his skill on them.

Ava is still working on her skills. She remembers key tricks to riding the whoops. She keeps her weight back. The front of her bike lifts over each whoop. She takes them one at a time. Her legs bend. The balls of her feet are on the pedals. The springs in the fork absorb the shock. Ava smiles as she turns the last corner. The updates to the bike worked well. Ava has a great first practice lap.

CHAPTER 4

Tough Competition

Lily sat in the stands. It was the second-to-last round of the 2018 motocross season. There are twelve rounds in the Lucas Oil Pro Motocross Championship. It was hot outside. But Lily didn't care. Her favorite racer was competing. His name was Aaron Plessinger. Plessinger had won a supercross championship earlier that year.

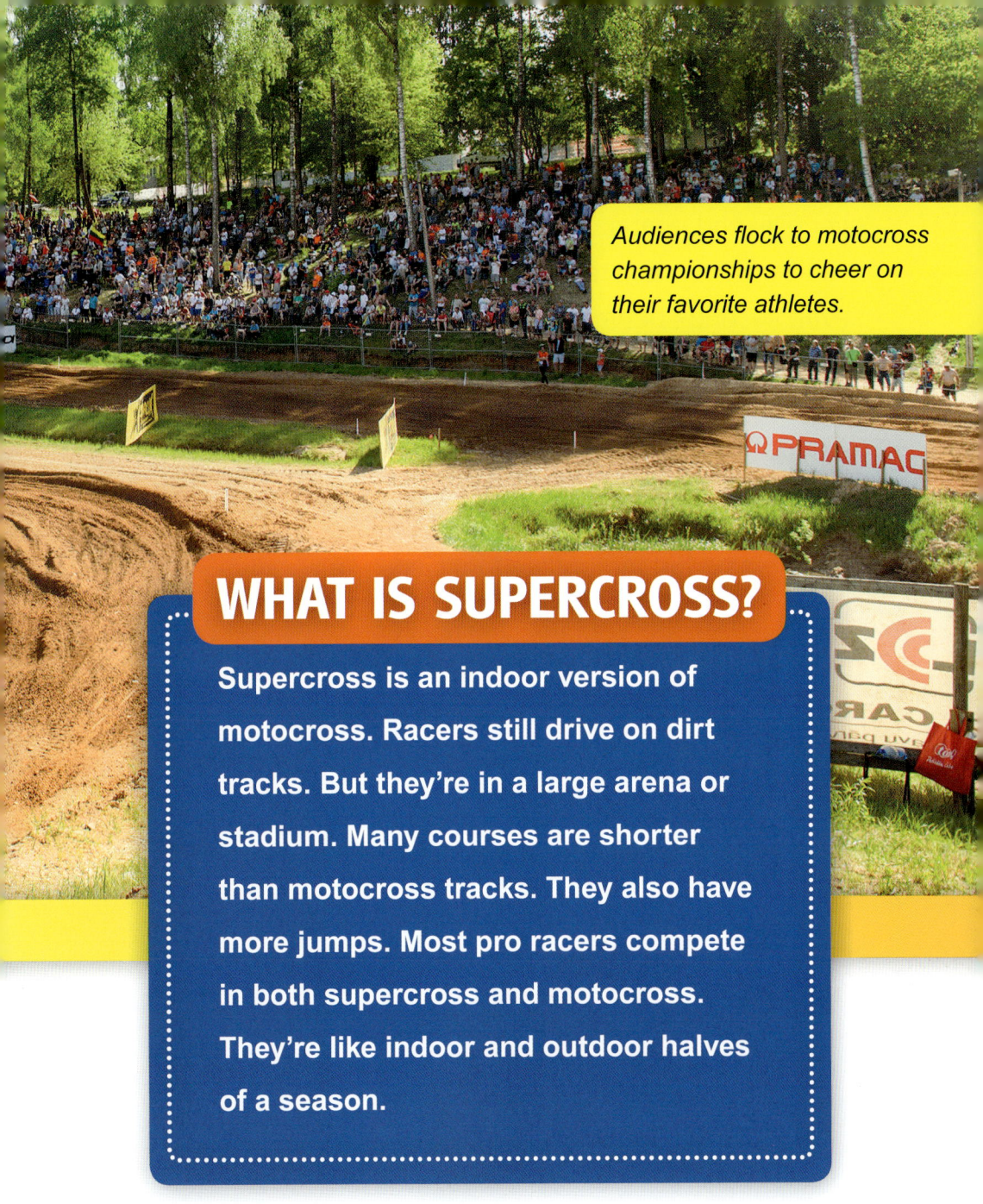

Audiences flock to motocross championships to cheer on their favorite athletes.

WHAT IS SUPERCROSS?

Supercross is an indoor version of motocross. Racers still drive on dirt tracks. But they're in a large arena or stadium. Many courses are shorter than motocross tracks. They also have more jumps. Most pro racers compete in both supercross and motocross. They're like indoor and outdoor halves of a season.

And he already had the most points this motocross season. The race began. Plessinger sped to the first corner. He got the holeshot! He pumped his fist. Lily cheered.

For thirty-five minutes, Plessinger powered through deep dirt. He flew over hills and jumps. He crossed the finish line. The next racer was almost seven seconds behind. Plessinger won the **moto**! There would be one more moto that day. But he had enough points to finish the season. He was the 2018 champion!

Lily was a big motocross fan. Her brother raced as an amateur. She went to his races. That's how she got into the sport. They also watched races together. There are international championships. People from different countries compete.

FUN FACT
In 2019, Aaron Plessinger began racing in the 450cc class.

Motocross and supercross fans can attend professional and amateur competitions around the world.

25

Lily and her brother went to the 2018 Motocross of Nations race. It was held in the United States. Plessinger competed there, too. He didn't win. But he raced hard. He faced tough competition from around the world.

The right motocross cycle is essential for aspiring professional racers.

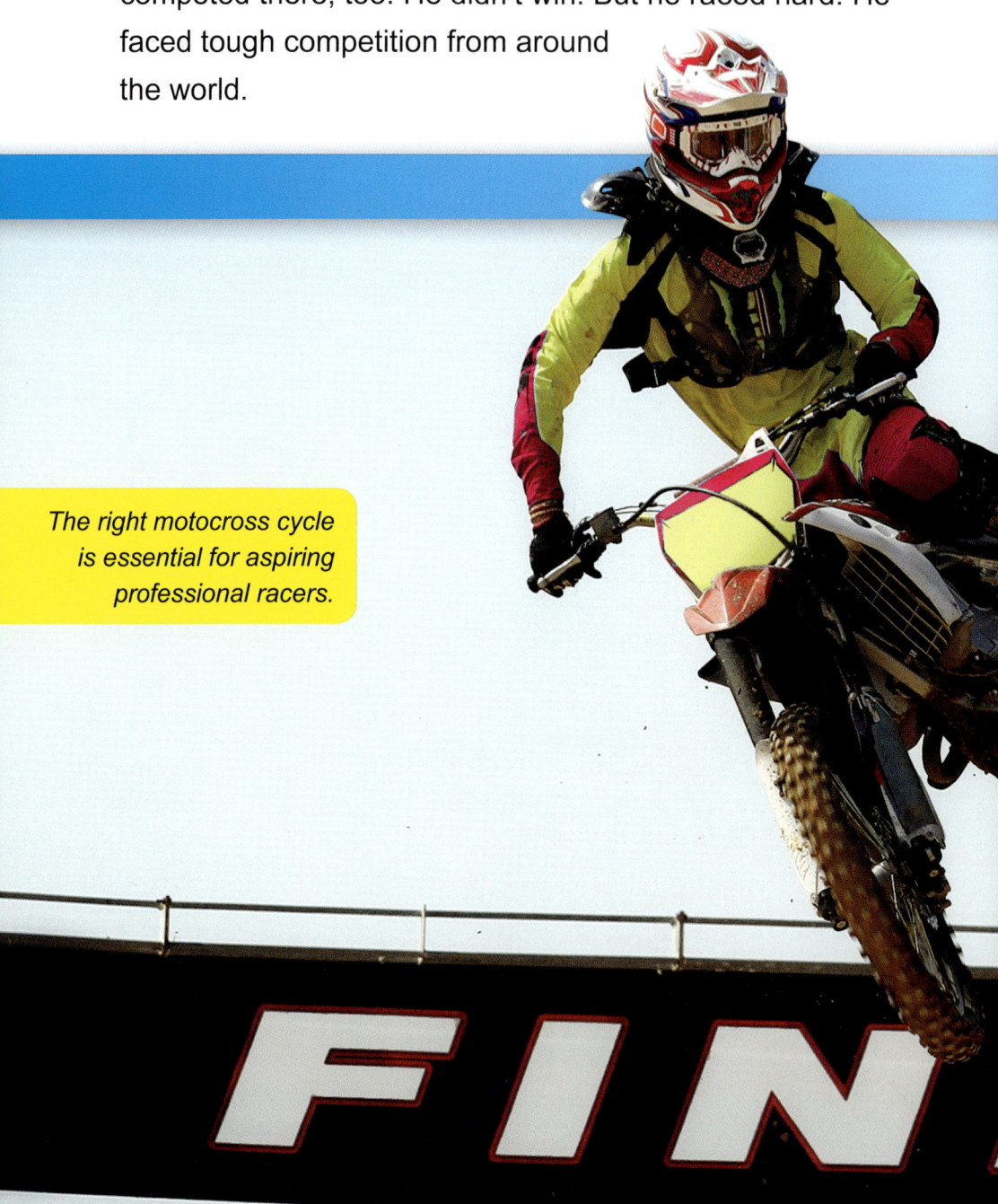

Lily's brother had a powerful new motocross cycle. It was lightweight and fast. Her brother zoomed over whoops. He veered around turns. With the new bike, he could go pro soon. He might even race Aaron Plessinger one day. Lily couldn't wait.

BEYOND
THE BOOK

After reading the book, it's time to think about what you learned. Try the following exercises to jumpstart your ideas.

THINK

THAT'S NEWS TO ME. Aaron Plessinger won the 2018 motocross championship. Consider how news sources might be able to fill in more detail on the event. What new information could be found in news articles? Where could you go to find those news sources?

CREATE

SHARPEN YOUR RESEARCH SKILLS. The book describes the history of motocross racing. Where could you go in the library, or who could you talk to, to find more information about motocross history? Create a research plan by writing a paragraph that details these next steps for research.

SHARE

SUM IT UP. Write a paragraph that summarizes the important points from the whole book. Remember to write the summary in your own words—don't just copy from the text. Next, share your paragraph with a classmate. Does the classmate have any feedback on the summary or additional questions about motocross cycles?

GROW

DRAWING CONNECTIONS. Create a diagram that shows and explains connections between motocross cycles and motocross competitions. How does learning about motocross competitions help you better understand motocross cycles?

RESEARCH NINJA

Visit *www.ninjaresearcher.com/0608* to learn how to take your research skills and book report writing to the next level!

RESEARCH

DIGITAL LITERACY TOOLS

SEARCH LIKE A PRO
Learn about how to use search engines to find useful websites.

FACT OR FAKE?
Discover how you can tell a trusted website from an untrustworthy resource.

TEXT DETECTIVE
Explore how to zero in on the information you need most.

SHOW YOUR WORK
Research responsibly—learn how to cite sources.

WRITE

GET TO THE POINT
Learn how to express your main ideas.

PLAN OF ATTACK
Learn prewriting exercises and create an outline.

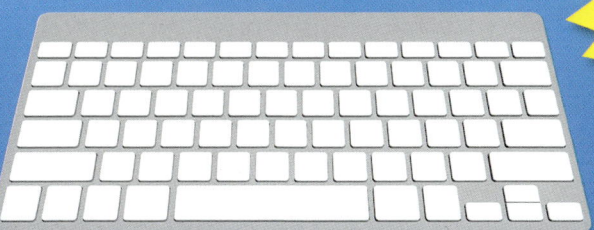

DOWNLOADABLE REPORT FORMS

29

Further Resources

BOOKS

Adamson, Thomas K. *Motocross Racing*. Bellwether Media, 2016.

Hinote Lanier, Wendy. *Dirt Bikes*. Focus Readers, 2017.

Shaffer, Lindsay. *Motocross Cycles*. Bellwether Media, 2019.

WEBSITES

FACTSURFER

Factsurfer.com gives you a safe, fun way to find more information.

1. Go to www.factsurfer.com.
2. Enter "Motocross Cycles" into the search box and click 🔍.
3. Select your book cover to see a list of related websites.

Glossary

amateur: An amateur is someone, such as an athlete, who is not paid for doing an activity. Amateur competitions can prepare racers for the professional level.

chassis: The chassis is the frame of a vehicle. Motocross cycles need a strong chassis that is also lightweight.

moto: A moto is one race in a motocross competition. Aaron Plessinger raced in two motos on the day he won the 2018 motocross championship.

motocross: Motocross is a type of dirt bike race done on closed courses made of rough dirt. Motocross tracks have big jumps and obstacles.

spokes: Spokes are the bars that support the shape of wheels. If the spokes of a motocross cycle snap, they could damage the wheel or tire.

suspension: The suspension of a vehicle is its system for absorbing shock from a road or track's hills and bumps. A tight suspension system is important for motocross cycles because they ride over high jumps.

terrain: Terrain is the physical features of land. Rough terrain is used for motocross courses.

throttle: The throttle is a lever on the handlebar that controls the gas flow. Tim twisted the throttle to give his motocross cycle gas during the race.

traction: Traction is something's grip on a surface, especially a tire on a road or track. Knobby tires help improve motocross cycles' traction.

Index

Carmichael, Ricky, 16, 21
chassis, 9, 17, 18

Dungey, Ryan, 8
Dye, Edison, 14

engines, 5, 9, 17, 18

Harley-Davidson, 12
headlights, 18
holeshot, 7, 23
Honda, 12

jumps, 7, 18, 21, 23, 24

kickstarter, 4

Lucas Oil Pro Motocross Championship, 22

moto, 24
Motocross of Nations, 26–27
motorcycles, 10–11, 14, 15

Plessinger, Aaron, 22–24, 25, 26–27

spokes, 9, 18
supercross, 22, 23
suspensions, 13, 17, 18, 21

throttle, 4, 9
tires, 4, 7, 9, 18, 21

whoops, 21, 27
World War II, 11

PHOTO CREDITS

The images in this book are reproduced through the courtesy of: Vytautas Kielaitis/Shutterstock Images, front cover (bike); OksanaNizienko/Shutterstock Images, front cover (background); Toa55/Shutterstock Images, pp. 3, 26–27; sportpoint/Shutterstock Images, pp. 4–5; Luti/Shutterstock Images, pp. 6–7; Kolbakova Olga/Shutterstock Images, p. 7; Warren Price Photography/Shutterstock Images, p. 8; TinoFotografie/Shutterstock Images, p. 9; Andrey 69/Shutterstock Images, pp. 10–11; colin13362/Shutterstock Images, p. 11; National Motor Museum Heritage Images/Newscom, p. 13; solepsizm/Shutterstock Images, p. 12 (top); tdee photo cm/Shutterstock Images, p. 12 (bottom); StockphotoVideo/Shutterstock Images, pp. 14–15; Sokolov Viktor/Shutterstock Images, p. 16; EvrenKalinbacak/Shutterstock Images, p. 17 (bike); Red Line Editorial, p. 17 (chart); ChickiBam/iStockphoto, p. 19; Studio 72/Shutterstock Images, pp. 20–21; Gints Ivuskans/Shutterstock Images, pp. 22–23; MuratOzcelik/Shutterstock Images, p. 24; tarczas/Shutterstock Images, pp. 24–25, 30.

ABOUT THE AUTHOR

Emma Huddleston enjoys reading and swing dancing. She lives in the Twin Cities with her husband.